MISSING MOGGY MYSTERY

MARGARET RYAN
ILLUSTRATED BY NICOLA SLATER

Hodder
Children's
Books

a division of Hodder Headline Limited

For Rebecca, with love –
Margaret Ryan

JF
1207926

Text copyright © 2002 Margaret Ryan
Illustrations copyright © 2002 Nicola Slater

First published in Great Britain in 2002
by Hodder Children's Books

A Catalogue record for this book is available from the British Library

ISBN 0 340 81706 2

Printed and bound in Great Britain by
Bookmarque Ltd., Croydon, Surrey

Hodder Children's Books
A division of Hodder Headline Limited
338 Euston Road, London NW1 3BH

Some other books by Margaret Ryan . . .

Hover Boy:

1: Fizzy Feet
2: Beat the Bully

For younger readers . . .

The Canterbury Tales
1: The Big Sister's Tale
2: The Little Brother's Tale
3: The Little Sister's Tale

For older readers . . .

Operation Boyfriend

published by Hodder Children's Books

CHAPTER ONE

Oscar Smith had a problem. Not a little problem, like goofy teeth or moose breath. Not a medium-sized problem, like a large conk or exceedingly loud burping, but a big problem. Big enough to change his life. Oscar's problem was that he could hover. Three feet into the air. Even higher if he put his mind to it.

Oscar always knew when the hovering was about to begin. A faint feeling of fizziness would start in his feet and he'd rise – sometimes slowly, sometimes quickly – three feet into the air. Not to be recommended in a low-ceilinged room, or on a bus, or in the presence of people likely to faint, like his teacher. Miss Cheevers had, in his old school, when she first saw Oscar hover in the gym. She'd collapsed like a large saggy beanbag, and, when she'd recovered, reported Oscar to Mr Robertson, the head teacher. He had sent for Oscar's parents immediately.

"Do you know that Oscar can hover?" he had asked.

"Oh yes. But he's a good boy really," said his mum.

Oscar's twin sisters, Evie and Angie, would definitely have disagreed with this. They thought he was a weirdo and told him so. Often.

But Mr Robertson hadn't thought that his school could cope with a weirdo . . . er . . . hoverer, so Oscar had been sent to the School Of Greatly Gifted Youth or S.O.G.G.Y., as it was known. Oscar loved it there.

At S.O.G.G.Y., almost everyone
had a special gift, as Madame Estella,
the head teacher, called it.

Oscar's best friends at his new
school were Gnatalie, who couldn't
spell but had x-ray vision, and Wibbly,
who could read minds as well as comics.
Banger McGrath was not Oscar's best
friend. He was no one's best friend.
He was the head boy – only because
his father owned the school – but had
no special gifts. He was at S.O.G.G.Y.
to try to learn some, and to keep an
eye on what went on there. He was only
good at bullying the other children,
and pinching their sweets.

But, aside from Banger, Oscar was
happy. He was happy that his hovering
wasn't a secret any more. He was happy
that he could hover into the air at
S.O.G.G.Y. and no one thought it
strange. Sometimes he had to do his

school work hovering halfway up the classroom wall, leaning on top of a tall cupboard, but no one batted an eyelid. At his last school, he'd had to clamp his legs round the legs of his desk whenever he felt the faint fizziness in his feet, and carry pockets full of small pebbles to try to weight himself down.

Oscar lay in bed thinking about it. Thinking about how his life had changed. Thinking about the challenge of being able to hover. Thinking about the freedom. Then the faint feeling of fizziness started in his feet and he hovered horizontally into the air and his duvet fell off. He had to do a funny little backward flip to get himself upright. Upright, but still three feet above the ground.

What time was it anyway? Oscar looked at his digital alarm. Two minutes to six. Oscar had set his alarm for six o'clock to get into the bathroom first. If his twin sisters got in before him there was never any hot water left, towels were sodden, and mysterious footprints appeared in the white powder which covered the bathroom floor. Oscar was sure his sisters threw their talc up in the air, and walked about underneath it.

A family breakfast was a recipe for disaster, too. The twins always bagged the best cereal, his mum always burnt the toast, and his dad always had to hit the smoke alarm with a brush to get it to stop. It was chaos. So, since Oscar liked a hot shower, some decent breakfast cereal (or, if he was lucky, some unburnt toast covered in his favourite chocolate spread), he set his alarm for early. That way he could hover about in peace.

He switched off his alarm before it had a chance to ring and hovered along to the bathroom. He was just cleaning his teeth and aiming his spit carefully into the basin – not easy while hanging in the air – when the faint feeling of fizziness went away, and he bumped down on to the floor. Unfortunately the twins had left their bar of Gorgeous Girls Beauty Soap lying there. Unfortunately Oscar slid on it, shot across the bathroom floor, and hit his elbow on the toilet.

"Ow!" He stifled a yell in case he woke the others, and got into the shower. The hot water was just taking the sting out of his elbow when the faint feeling of fizziness in his feet started again, and he shot up into the air, and banged his head on the shower rose.

"Ow!" Oscar stifled another yell, and folded himself into a crouch position under the shower.

The hot water was just taking the sting out of his head when the faint feeling of fizziness disappeared completely and he fell into the shower tray, banging his knee.

"Oh I give up," muttered Oscar and climbed out. "I'm probably clean enough now, anyway."

He dressed in his old jeans and a jumper – school uniform wasn't worn at S.O.G.G.Y., except for Banger McGrath who wore his father's old school

11

uniform – and went downstairs.

The house was still quiet. Oscar loved this time of day. He could hear all sorts of sounds he wasn't normally aware of. He could hear Grandma Jemima's old clock ticking, he could hear the fridge humming ("Though it only knows one tune," giggled Oscar). And he could hear his cereal crick-cracking as he poured the milk on.

He was just listening to it when the faint feeling of fizziness started in his feet again, and he shot three feet up into the air and poured the milk all over the kitchen table.

"Oh, no," said Oscar, and hovered away to find a cloth to mop up the mess. He was just reaching down into the sink when the faint feeling of fizziness disappeared, he went down with a thump, and hit his nose on the kitchen tap. His nose bled

and he had to stuff bits of paper
towel up it to stop the blood dripping
into his cereal and turning the milk
pink.

"This," muttered Oscar, "is just
not my day. Talk about getting out
of bed on the wrong side. Still, I don't
suppose things can get much worse."

But they did . . .

CHAPTER TWO

Oscar's hover, walk, hover, walk to school was hardly noticed. Most people were too busy running for trains or buses to notice a rather skinny, freckle-faced boy whose feet didn't touch the ground. Those who did notice checked their glasses or their pulses, and thought they must be seeing things.

Oscar's mind was on Madame Estella's cat, Mystic Mog. He had recently found out that Mystic Mog could speak. Not cat-speak like *purr* or *miaow* or *hiss*, but human-speak like "Hullo, Oscar" and "Well done, Oscar".

Oscar rounded the corner of Beacham Road and smiled as S.O.G.G.Y came into view. He loved the crumbling old house with its overgrown garden and its creaky iron gates. He loved the way the school door was always slightly open, making it seem both welcoming and mysterious at the same time. He loved the way Mystic Mog always sat at the top of the short flight of steps leading up to the front door.

But wait a minute . . . Oscar blinked and looked again. This morning there was no Mystic Mog. No blackish, brownish, whitish with a little bit of orange cat delicately cleaning her paws there . . . Oscar's tummy gave a funny little wobble.

"I don't like this," he muttered. "Something's wrong."

He ran up the steps, then the faint

feeling of fizziness started in his feet and he hovered his way through the narrow passageways, past the panel of old-fashioned bells that no longer worked, till he got to Madame Estella's room.

He knocked and hovered.

"Please come in." Madame Estella's voice sounded a little wavery. "Oh Oscar," she said. "I'm so pleased to see you. Something dreadful has happened. Mystic Mog is missing."

Oscar nodded. "I knew something was wrong when she wasn't on the top step. But she can't have gone far. I'll help you look for her."

"I've looked everywhere I can think of," said Madame Estella, running her fingers through her hair that was piled higgledy-piggledy on top of her head. As usual it had at least three pencils stuck in it. "I only came back here to

check she hadn't been shut up in
any of the classrooms."

"You go and look everywhere
again," said Oscar, "and I'll hover up
and look over all the high walls and
up in the trees in case she's got stuck
somewhere."

"Thank you, Oscar," said Madame
Estella. "You're very kind. I know you've
always been very fond of Mystic Mog."

Oscar nodded and hovered away.
He didn't want to upset Madame
Estella any more, but he didn't like this.
Mystic Mog wouldn't just disappear.

He searched the entire neighbourhood.
It was full of old houses with big
gardens and high walls. Many of the
houses had been split into flats and,
as people left for work, he got some
very strange looks when they spotted
his head suddenly appearing over
their wall.

17

"Go away" and "Clear off" were
some of the less rude things that
were yelled at him. Oscar stuck out
his tongue and kept looking. But
though he looked over all the high
walls and hovered up into all the trees,
there was no sign of Mystic Mog.

Madame Estella had had no luck
either.

"Where on earth can she be, Oscar?" she asked, pacing up and down her room. "She never goes off. Not since the night she arrived on my doorstep after the—" and she stopped and looked at Oscar. "After the U.F.O. sighting."

Oscar's eyes opened wide. "So she might be another one," he said.

Oscar, Gnatalie and Wibbly had recently found out that nearly all the children in the school had been born on the same nights that Madame Estella had seen mysterious green lights in the sky. And nearly all the children had special gifts.

Oscar often wondered about that. Could the gifts have been sent to them by an alien life form? Did the aliens have these gifts themselves and were going to communicate at some point? Oscar just didn't know.

What he did know was that the only child at S.O.G.G.Y. not to have a special gift was Banger McGrath. *His* birthday did not match up with any of the U.F.O. sightings. But there was one other with a special gift. Mystic Mog.

Oscar cleared his throat and looked at Madame Estella. "I know that Mystic Mog can speak," he said.

Madame Estella nodded. "Mog told me she had spoken to you, Oscar. I've kept her speaking a secret from everyone. I was afraid, if it were known, she might be kidnapped by some horrible people and used to make money. Now I'm afraid that's exactly what's happened." And Madame Estella's cornflower blue eyes watered dangerously.

"She said a very strange thing to me several times last week," she went on. "It was so strange I wrote it down, but I wasn't sure what to do about it."

She went to the top drawer of her desk and took out a notebook and showed it to Oscar. On the first page she had written . . .

DANGER DANGER
BUT NOT FROM
A STRANGER

"What can it mean?"

"Don't know," said Oscar. "But I'll find out. Can I tell Gnatalie and Wibbly about Mystic Mog being able to speak? With their special gifts they'll be able to help."

Madame Estella nodded.

"Don't worry," said Oscar. "They're very good at keeping secrets. We'll soon find Mystic Mog.

CHAPTER THREE

Oscar hovered along to his classroom
to find Gnatalie and Wibbly. Like
Oscar they were usually in school early.
But not today. Today there was no
Gnatalie or Wibbly, but Mr Periwinkle,
the caretaker, was halfway up a ladder
taking books down from a high shelf.

"Oh hullo, Oscar," he said. "You're
the very one to help me. These shelves
are coming away from the wall with
the weight of all these books. Could
you help me lift down the books and
save my old legs?"

Mr Periwinkle had white hair and
pink cheeks and was one of the nicest

men Oscar had ever met. He never complained about footballs going up on to the school roof. He never complained about muddy boots all over the hall floor. And he never put salt on the best slides. He had a kind word for everybody.

"How are your mum and dad?" he asked Oscar. "Still working hard in the dairy and the supermarket?"

"Yes," said Oscar. "They're both having to work extra hours just now because there's flu about, so I had to do the shopping yesterday. It took me ages. My hovering came on in the supermarket and all the old ladies thought it was great, and got me to get them things down from the high shelves."

Mr Periwinkle smiled.

"And what about your sisters, Evie and Angie? Still going to be beauticians when they grow up?"

"Uh huh," said Oscar. "They wanted to try out a face pack on me last night. Something they'd made up out of oatmeal and honey. Imagine wearing sticky porridge on your face. But I hovered away sharpish.

"They got Dad, though. He was having a quiet snooze in the chair after work and they covered his face in the lumpy goo they'd mixed up. Gave him the fright of his life when he snored and a bit fell into his

mouth and he swallowed it. He wasn't too pleased about the cucumber eye patches either. Neither was Mum. The cucumber was for the salad."

Mr Periwinkle laughed.

"I wish I had a funny family like that," he said.

He screwed a few more nails into the shelves, and Oscar helped him put all the books back, just as the faint feeling of fizziness in his feet disappeared, and he bumped down to the floor.

Oscar had just helped Mr Periwinkle clear away the step ladders when the rest of the class started to arrive.

"Hi, Hover Boy," said Peter Purbright, otherwise known as Big-ears, because of his extra-acute hearing. "I hear you nearly had a porridge face pack last night?"

Oscar laughed. Big-ears could hear a pin drop a hundred metres away.

Then a large orange tree came in on two legs. Carrying it was Wanda Fonda.

"Hi, Oscar," she said. "How do you like my orange tree? I worked really hard on it for homework. It was just a pip last night. Have an orange, if you like."

Oscar grinned and plucked a ripe fruit. Wanda could grow plants just by looking at them and saying "Grow, plant, grow". She could make ears and noses grow too, so it was as well not to annoy her.

Gnatalie and Wibbly were last so Oscar didn't have time to talk to them before the first lesson, or discovery, as it was called at S.O.G.G.Y.

"This morning . . ." said Mr Blister, nicknamed Rumble, because his tum always did. "This morning, ladies and gentlemen, I want you to write a short paragraph about your family. I want you to make it as interesting as possible."

Oh no, thought Oscar. What can I say about my family that's interesting? Mum and Dad work hard, but that's not really interesting. Evie and Angie are pains in the neck, but that's not

really interesting. Then he remembered
how Mr Periwinkle had laughed when
he told him about the honey and
porridge face pack.

"I'll write about that," he said
to himself, and took out his notebook.
That was when he noticed a jagged
edge where a page had been torn out.
How did that happen, he wondered, but
thought no more about it as he began
to write his story.

Then he sat back and wondered
what Gnatalie and Wibbly would
write about. Their families were
really interesting. Gnatalie's parents
were famous sculptors and Wibbly's
mum had a cookery programme on
the telly. They would have loads to
write about.

After about fifteen minutes Mr
Blister said, "Rest from your labours,
ladies and gentlemen" – he was always

saying odd things like that – "and
we'll hear what you've written."

"I bet mine's the best," hissed
Banger McGrath in Oscar's ear.
"My dad's just got a brand new Roller.
I've written about that. What does
your dad drive? I bet it's a milk float!"

Oscar said nothing. Somehow the
honey and porridge face pack didn't
seem so interesting any more.

Mr Blister chose Gnatalie to read
out her paragraph first.

"I don't think I've spelled it very
well," she told Mr Blister. Gnatalie's
spelling was nearly as bad as her
parents'. They hadn't really meant to
spell her name the same as the insect.

"Just read it out, Gnatalie,"
encouraged Mr Blister. "We can't *hear*
the spelling."

Gnatalie began. "I was nearly late
for school this morning because the

kitchen ceiling fell down. Mum and Dad are making a new sculpture called Shades of Grey. It's got all kinds of grey things in it. They took the old grey socks I had at my last school and my T-shirt that went a bit grey in the wash. I didn't mind that, but they also took some of the grey slates off the roof, and the rain got in, and the kitchen ceiling fell down into my cornflakes, and made my hair all grey. I expect they would have taken a bit of that too if I hadn't left quickly."

Oscar looked at Gnatalie's hair. Sure enough it was a funny grey colour, like she'd gone elderly all of a sudden.

"Well done, Gnatalie," said Mr Blister. "That was interesting."

Mr Blister called on Wibbly next.

"I was nearly late for school this morning too because my mum held up the number nine bus. Not like a highway mum. Get it? Highway mum! But with my sandwiches. Mum makes exotic casseroles for a living and I get the leftovers in my sandwiches. They looked especially horrible this morning so I sneaked out without them.

"But Mum noticed, and held up the bus till she had given them to me. The bus driver wasn't pleased and gave Mum a telling off. She told him he was only cross because he ate all the wrong things, and that tomorrow, she would bring him a sandwich with a special filling in it, to calm him down. I'm going to walk to school tomorrow."

"Well, I always get a lift to school," sneered Banger McGrath, and launched into his story without being asked. "My dad," he said, "has a brand new, state of the art, top of the range, silver Rolls-

Royce. It's got leather upholstery, shiny wheels and a lot of very expensive dials that tell you things, like . . . well, *lots* of things." And he stopped and smirked all round.

"Is that it, Banger?" asked Mr Blister. Banger nodded.

"Thank you," said Mr Blister.

Banger scowled. He was sure Mr Blister would have said his was the best.

Then it was Oscar's turn. He stood up, but at that moment the faint feeling of fizziness in his feet came back, and he rose slowly into the air.

"Oh, Hover Boy," said Mr Blister. "I can see this is going to be a tall tale . . . "

Oscar finally managed to come down to earth for the last discovery that morning. It was Metal-bending. Not with glowing hot coals and a great hairy blacksmith. Not with a beam of light and a laser technician, but with Titch Maguire, the littlest girl in the school.

Mr Blister brought her along to Oscar's classroom. He also brought along a suitcase that clanked. He put it up on his desk and turned to the class.

"For any of you who don't know her," he said, "this is Titch. She is our youngest student and she's going to demonstrate her special gift to you today. Her ability to bend metal is remarkable, so I must ask you to search your pockets and your bags, remove any metal objects you don't want bent, and put them outside the classroom door. Just in case."

"Bending metal," Oscar heard Banger mutter. "Ridiculous. Look at the size of her. She's so small if she bent over she'd disappear completely."

Oscar searched his pockets.
He had a crumpled hanky, an old
bit of chewing-gum and a ten-pence
piece. He decided to leave the ten-
pence piece on his desk to see what
happened. Wibbly put his special
pen outside the door and Gnatalie
put out the metal pencil box her
dad had made her.

When everyone was back in
their seats, Mr Blister opened up the
suitcase. Inside was an assortment of
cutlery and candlesticks. He laid them
out on a table at the front of the room.

"Now, gather round, ladies and
gentlemen," he said. "And watch
carefully."

The class gathered round. Only
Banger stayed in his seat. "I bet
nothing happens. Who wants to bet
me nothing happens. What about
you, Hover Boy. Want to bet that

ten pence? I've got a two-pound
coin in my pocket. I'll bet you that."

Oscar ignored him and Mr
Blister muttered "Silly boy," at which
everyone else giggled.

Banger grunted and banged
about at his desk, but no one paid
any attention. They were too busy
watching Titch Maguire at work.
She said nothing, just picked up
spoon after spoon and stroked it
gently. The spoons all bent over.

Metal
Bending

So did the candlesticks. Then she stroked them the opposite way and bent them back again.

"Wow," said Oscar. "That's fantastic. I wonder if you could fix my bike? I hovered into the air while I was riding it and it ran into a wall and got bent."

"And my dad bent the metal bumper on his vintage car in last month's rally," said Big-ears. "He'd love to meet you."

"So would my parents," said Gnatalie. "You would be a great help to them with their sculptures."

"Thank you," whispered Titch and smiled shyly.

"Thank *you*, Titch," smiled Mr Blister, "for that splendid demonstration. Now, I'll take you and the suitcase back to your classroom." He picked up the suitcase and went to the door with Titch.

"Huh, good riddance," muttered Banger, and stood up and waved. "Bye bye, stupid little girlie."

Titch turned and gave Banger a penetrating stare, then she followed Mr Blister out of the room.

"That was a really stupid trick," scoffed Banger, "and you all fell for it. And you didn't need to put things outside the door. Look, the ten pence on Hover Boy's desk isn't even bent, and my two-pound coin is" – and he took it out of his pocket – "bent?"

And he sat down heavily on his seat and crashed to the floor as the metal legs buckled and gave way.

"*Now* who looks stupid," grinned Oscar. "And by the way, Banger, that's two pounds you owe me!"

CHAPTER FOUR

"You're *serious*? Mystic Mog really can talk?" said Gnatalie and Wibbly, when Oscar finally managed to speak to them on their own at lunchtime.

They had gone to their favourite meeting place at the back of the school. A secret path round the side of the bramble patch led to a little clearing where a fallen oak tree made a good place to sit.

Oscar nodded, his mouth full of corned beef sandwich.

"I'm not really surprised," said Wibbly. "I knew that's what you'd been thinking for some time. I've watched

Mystic Mog carefully, but she's never spoken to me. She must have chosen you specially, Oscar. Cats choose their humans very carefully."

Oscar smiled and shared his sandwiches with Wibbly. As usual Wibbly had fed his to the large crows that gathered in a row each day, waiting. Crows would eat anything.

"Mystic Mog arrived at Madame Estella's front door on the night of one of the U.F.O. sightings," said Oscar. "Madame Estella had just come back from spotting the U.F.O. over the town hall, and there was the cat, sitting on her doorstep."

"Wow, so she's like all the rest of us – except Banger, of course," said Gnatalie. "*She's* connected with a U.F.O. sighting, too. Her special gift is that she can speak."

"That's what's worrying Madame

Estella. She thinks someone may have heard Mystic Mog speak and kidnapped – or catnapped – her to make money. Some people would pay a lot to hear a talking cat."

"But Mystic Mog chooses the people she speaks to," pointed out Wibbly. "She doesn't chatter away all the time when just anybody can hear, otherwise we'd have heard her. Then there's this odd message she gave Madame Estella. What was it? 'Danger danger but not from a stranger'. That could mean it's someone Madame Estella knows."

"That could mean half the town," said Oscar. "She talks to everyone and everyone likes her."

"Except the person who's nicked her cat," said Gnatalie.

"We'll search the neighbourhood after school again," said Oscar. "Surely

with three of us looking we'll soon
find Mystic Mog."

But they didn't.

Oscar looked over the walls again
and hovered up into the trees. It was
rather nice sitting up there in among
the branches looking down on the
world. He could see why cats liked it.
But though he came across various
other cats, and the odd, annoyed
squirrel, he didn't find Mystic Mog.

Gnatalie looked through all the walls of the nearby houses. She saw people drinking coffee and children watching telly. She saw other cats, but she didn't see Mystic Mog.

Wibbly went with her and read the minds of the people in the houses, but they were either thinking about what to make for tea, trying to answer the questions on a TV quiz, or thinking about their football team. There was no one thinking about how to make money from a talking cat.

"Let's meet in our caravan den tonight," said Oscar, hovering down from his last tree, "and decide what to do next."

CHAPTER FIVE

"You're not going out into that caravan den tonight, are you?" Evie and Angie asked Oscar after tea. "It's freezing out there. You'll have icicles hanging from your nose, your face will turn blue and your ears will drop off."

Oscar sighed. The twins loved to exaggerate.

"Gnatalie, Wibby and I have something very important to discuss," he said.

"I heard of a woman once who spent the night in a caravan in the winter time, and when she woke up in the morning she was stuck to the side with ice. The fire brigade had to chip her off with axes," said Evie. "They nearly chopped her head off."

"And I heard of a boy who died in a caravan in the winter, and no one found him till he'd thawed out in the spring," said Angie.

"We won't die out there," said Oscar. "We're only in the back garden and we've got rugs."

"And tomato soup," said his mum and handed him a flask and some mugs.

"Oh, tomato soup!" said the twins. "We love tomato soup. Can we come?"

"No," said Oscar. "This is a private meeting in a private den."

"Don't be too long," said Oscar's mum. "Then Dad take will Gnatalie and Wibbly home."

The three friends sat in their
den, round their torch light, huddled
in their tartan rugs. Their breath
made white puffs in the air, and
their shadows strange shapes on
the wall.

"This is spooky," said Gnatalie.

"Eerie," whispered Wibbly.

"Oooooooo," said Oscar.

But the ghostly "Oooooooo" turned to a human "Owwww" as the faint feeling of fizziness in his feet started and he shot very quickly three feet up into the air, and banged his head on the caravan roof.

"I'm definitely going to get a crash helmet," he said. "And elbow pads," he added, as the faint feeling of fizziness disappeared, and he fell to the floor.

"You should learn to control your hovering, Hover Boy," grinned Gnatalie.

"That's what I'm trying to do in school," said Oscar. "It seems that when I really need to hover, I can. Like searching for Mystic Mog this

morning. It's when I don't need to
hover that it's unpredictable. That
makes it tricky."

"Finding Mystic Mog's another
tricky thing," said Wibbly, taking a
big gulp of his tomato soup and
gaining a red moustache. "How are
we going to do that? We've searched
everywhere."

"What about the cat and dog
home?" said Gnatalie. "We could try
there."

"Or we could put an ad in the
paper," said Oscar. "Something like:
'Lost: One cat. Answers to the name
of Mystic Mog.'"

"You'd have to describe her,"
said Gnatalie. "'Lost: One blackish,
brownish, whitish, with a little bit
of orange cat, with a silver bell on
a blue collar. Answers to the name of
Mystic Mog.'"

"She's not easy to describe, is she?" said Wibbly.

"No, but she'll be easy to spot," said Oscar. "Tomorrow's Saturday. We'll go to the cat and dog home in the morning and see if Mystic Mog is there."

Suddenly there was a thump on the caravan wall.

"Is there anybody there?" moaned a voice, very like Evie's.

"Knock once for yes, twice for no," moaned a voice, very like Angie's.

Two heads covered in white sheets appeared at the caravan window and the sound of clanking buckets was heard.

"We are the ghosts of wild, woolly winter," went on both voices. "Coming to freeze you to a long, lingering death."

Oscar opened the caravan door
and shone the torch on his two sisters.
"That wasn't spooky at all," he said.
"Huh! You knew it was us all the
time," they said, taking off their white
sheets. They'd been playing beauty

schools again, and, in the torch light, Oscar could see their green hair, purple eye shadow and blue frosted lips.

"Aaaargh!" he yelled, pretending to shake with fright. "Now looking at the real you, that *is* scary!"

CHAPTER SIX

Next morning Gnatalie, Wibbly and Oscar caught the bus to the cat and dog home. The bus driver was very chatty.

"Lost your dog, have you?" he said, as they paid their fare. "Ours is always running off. I tell the wife I'd run off too if all I got to eat was dried biscuits and water."

"It's our cat we've lost," said Oscar. "You haven't seen her? She's kind of blackish, brownish, whitish, with a little bit of orange, and answers to the name of Mystic Mog."

"Good name," said the bus driver.

"Can she tell the future? Haven't seen her but if she comes on my bus I'll tell her to go home."

"Do you often get animals on your bus?" asked Oscar.

The bus driver nodded. "I get all sorts on this bus. Had a pot-bellied piglet last week, and a twelve-foot boa constrictor called Blossom the week before that. Took up two seats she did, and didn't pay her fare. I didn't argue. You don't, with a boa constrictor."

The three friends went to the back of the bus where it was bumpiest.

"I love going over the speed bumps," said Wibbly.

"Me too," said Gnatalie.

"Wow," they said as they went over a big one, rather too fast.

Wibbly and Gnatalie bumped up and down. Oscar bumped up and

stayed there, hovering in a sitting
position above the seat.

"Oh no," he said. "I can't get
down. We'll be put off the bus for
mucking about."

But they weren't. No one
seemed to notice, and the faint
feeling of fizziness in Oscar's feet
went away just before their stop, and
he bumped down on to the seat.

They were just getting off the bus when the driver said, "That's a really good trick, that sitting-on-air thing. I can wiggle my ears and sing *Three Blind Mice* at the same time, but that sitting-on-air thing's really good."

The cat and dog home was very busy. Oscar had never seen so many cats and dogs in one place. Gnatalie couldn't take her eyes off the lost dogs. She had to stop and pat and chat to every one.

"Oh look," she kept saying. "Isn't she sweet? How could anyone abandon her?" Or, "Look at that sad little dog over there. He must be lost. I hope his owner claims him soon."

"Perhaps you should get a dog, Gnatalie," said Oscar.

"I'd love one," sighed Gnatalie. "But I'm at school all day and who'd look after it? Mum and Dad are hopeless. They forget I'm there half the time. A dog would have no chance. It wouldn't be fair."

"I'd like a cat," said Wibbly. "But we can't get one because Mum's terrified she'd get cat hairs in her cooking. I don't suppose hairy casseroles would be a good idea."

"Why don't you get a pet, Oscar?"

"It's difficult walking a dog from three feet up in the air," said Oscar. "And the twins would want to dress it up in ribbons and bows and paint its nails. Even if it was a he!"

Gnatalie and Wibbly nodded.

"It's rotten having to be sensible, isn't it?" said Gnatalie. "There should be a law that says sensible is just for grown-ups."

At the cat and dog home there were plenty of grown-ups looking

for lost pets. The three friends
recognized one of them immediately.
"Madame Estella!" they called.

"Oh hello, my dears," she said,
looking more untidy and distracted
than ever. "How good of you to
come. I've been here every day
since Mystic Mog disappeared, but

she's not here. There are lots of other poor lost creatures, but no Mog."

And Madame Estella's shoulders drooped and her eyes got watery again.

"We thought of an ad in the paper," said Oscar, and showed Madame Estella the one he'd written out.

"It's certainly worth a try," she said. "I'll come with you to the newspaper office right now. The sooner we get it in the better."

"Thing is," said Oscar, "I sometimes hover on the bus. I can't help it but it can be a bit embarrassing."

"Oh, we don't need to go on the bus," said Madame Estella. "We can all squeeze into James. He's over there."

And she pointed to an elderly Volkswagen Beetle which had been painted with silver stars and whirling planets.

"I had a lot of paint left over when I finished painting the stars and planets on my sitting-room ceiling," said Madame Estella, "so I painted James as well. Trouble is, I don't think he likes it. I think he preferred being plain boring blue. He's been a bit huffy since I painted him.

Sometimes he'll start first time, sometimes he won't. Let's hope he's in a good mood today. He doesn't like Saturday morning traffic."

The three friends mouthed, "Barking, but nice."

But James wasn't nice. He was in a stubborn mood. He started first time, but stopped at the first set of traffic lights, and wouldn't start again till he'd been pushed for half a mile. Then when they were all thoroughly puffed out, he roared into life, and took them to the newspaper office.

A bubble-gum blowing girl at the front desk took their ad.

"I'm sorry the ad's a bit odd," said Oscar. "Our cat's a bit difficult to describe."

"'S all right," said the girl. "We had an odd ad in last week too.

Someone selling a brand new scooter, in perfect condition, with no wheels. We get all sorts in here."

"That's the second time we've heard that today," grinned Oscar.

CHAPTER SEVEN

Several days passed and there were several replies to the ad. People came to the school clutching a variety of cats and kittens. Trouble was, some just abandoned them there and went off hurriedly, so one morning Oscar found Madame Estella in her study, knee deep in cats.

There were black cats, white cats, cats-that-had-been-in-a-fight cats, cats that were stripy and cats that were tabby, cats that were thin and cats that were flabby, but there was no Mystic Mog. No cat answering her description had been seen anywhere.

Oscar helped Madame Estella pile
all the cats into her old Beetle and
take them to the cat and dog home.
Mog still wasn't there either. The
friends got more and more worried,
and Madame Estella, who seemed
to be coming down with the flu,
got thinner and thinner. Then, one
morning at break, she called the
friends to her office.

"Thid was left on my doorstep thid morning," she snuffled and handed them a torn piece of paper. It was tied to Mystic Mog's collar.

> LEVE AN ENVILOP WIV A HUNDRID POUNDS BY THE SKOOL GATE AT FIVE O'CLOCK TOMOROW IF YOU WONT TO SEE YOUR CAT ALIVE AGEN

"That spelling's worse than mine," said Gnatalie.

"Who do we know whose spelling's worse than yours?" said Wibbly."

"Banger McGrath," said Oscar, and suddenly remembered the jagged edge in his notebook.

"Oh surely nod," croaked Madame Estella. "Banger's a bully like his fadder but surely he wouldn't have stolen Mystic Mod?"

63

"He'd do anything to try to get me into trouble," said Oscar, and told them about the torn-out page. "And remember what Mystic Mog said to you? 'Danger danger but not from a stranger.'"

Madame Estella blew her reddened nose and still looked doubtful.

"Tell you what," said Oscar. "I'll follow him home today, and see if I can find out anything. If there's nothing unusual then we'll have to think again."

For the rest of that day, Oscar kept a close eye on his rucksack with his notebook in it, but Banger did nothing, though he kept grinning at Oscar.

That's very suspicious, thought Oscar. He usually scowls.

Oscar stayed in school till he saw Banger leave, then followed him home.

At first it wasn't difficult. Banger
left such a trail of litter behind him.
Oscar counted three chocolate bar
wrappers, two sweet papers and an
apple core in the first ten minutes.
Oscar kept well back and simply
dodged into shop doorways or
gazed in shop windows whenever
Banger looked round.

He didn't mind looking in the
sweet shop or the pet shop window
but when he had to look into the
fashion shop window that was the
twins' favourite he could feel his ears
go bright red.

Then Banger crossed the road
and took a short cut across the park.
Oscar had to dodge behind trees to
keep out of sight.

"Good thing I'm skinny," said
Oscar, sliding behind a slender silver
birch when Banger stopped to snatch

a ball from a small boy. He teased the boy with it, holding it high above his head and wouldn't give it back until the boy's mother appeared. Then he kicked over a litter bin and ran off laughing.

"What a horror," muttered Oscar. "No wonder no one likes him." And he thought about what that must be like, and was almost sorry for Banger, till he saw him chasing some ducks.

"Quack quack quack," yelled Banger, flapping his arms and scattering the ducks in all directions.

"Quack quack quack," replied the ducks, and paddled furiously to the safety of the middle of the pond.

It was at that moment that Oscar felt the faint fizziness in his feet and he shot up into the air. Fortunately he was hiding behind an oak tree at the time. Unfortunately the oak

tree had some low-slung branches.
Oscar cracked his head on one of
them and had to do a funny little
backward flip to get himself up on
to a branch. Fortunately Banger
hadn't seen him. Unfortunately the
park keeper had.

"Get down from that tree, you
horrible boy," he yelled, hurrying
over. "Are you the one who's been
dropping litter all over my tidy park?
Are you the one that's been upsetting
the children and the ducks?"

"N-n-n-no, not me," said Oscar.

"Well, get down here this minute
till I get a proper look at you."

Oscar tried to get down from the
tree but the faint feeling of fizziness
was still there and he hovered in front of
the park keeper, three feet up in the air.

The park keeper rubbed his eyes.
"What the—"

"Sorry," said Oscar, and hovered away.

The park keeper sat down on the nearest bench and took of his glasses.

"Time I got new glasses," he said. "I'm starting to see things with this pair."

Oscar walked and hovered and hovered and walked all the way to Banger's house. It was a large modern house at the other side of the park. The house had high walls round it and a sign on the electronically-controlled gates saying . . .

FIERCE DOGS PATROLLING

Oscar listened for the sound of barking, but could hear nothing. He watched as Banger punched in a number on the key pad and the gates opened noiselessly.

"Bit different from the creaky gates at S.O.G.G.Y.," muttered Oscar.

Banger punched in another number on the key pad by the front door and it swung open too. Oscar had a quick glimpse of a marble floor

and thick rugs before Banger
disappeared and the door clicked
shut. Oscar kept out of sight behind the
high wall and thought about what to
do next.

I wonder what Banger will do
now that he's inside? he thought.
Change out of that horrible uniform
that belonged to his dad? Possibly.
Have something more to eat? Probably.
Watch T.V. or play a computer game?
Almost certainly.

Oscar waited for a few minutes
to give Banger time to settle, then
hovered up into the air and took
a quick peep over the wall. He saw
a neatly laid out garden, a fountain
splashing in a pond but no sign of
any large dogs. Then Banger
appeared from a back door.

Oscar slid down the wall till only
his mop of hair and his eyes showed.

He watched as Banger headed towards a small shed in the garden and disappeared inside. A few moments later Banger reappeared and hurried back to the house, carrying a small wicker hamper. Oscar couldn't see what was inside. "But I bet it's Mystic Mog," he muttered to himself.

Oscar watched all the windows on the ground floor for a few minutes till a movement caught his eye. Banger. He came into the sitting-room with the hamper and put it on the glass-topped coffee table. Then he sprawled over a large, black, leather sofa, picked up a remote control, and flicked on the television. He tried several channels but nothing seemed to interest him. He switched off the television and prowled round the room.

After a few moments he came back and opened up the hamper. He took out a cat and held it, at arm's length, by the scruff of the neck. Hiding behind the wall, Oscar took a deep breath.

Even at a distance he could plainly see the cat was blackish, brownish, whitish, with a little bit of orange. Very much like Mystic Mog.

"Found her," breathed Oscar
and sank slowly to the ground.

He raced home and phoned
Gnatalie and Wibbly.

"What a rotter Banger is," they both
said. "We must get Mystic Mog back
as soon as possible and teach Banger
a lesson."

"I'll phone Madame Estella, then
I'll try to work out how we'll do it,"
said Oscar, and hovered up and down
his bedroom thinking about it.

He was still thinking about it over
tea.

"What's the matter, Oscar?" said
his mum. "You're not eating. I thought
you liked bangers and mash."

"I do usually," said Oscar. But
the bangers reminded him too much
of a certain other Banger.

"Then we'll have yours if you

don't want them," said the twins,
and swiped them before he could
change his mind.

Oscar didn't care. He hovered
up into the air and worried about
getting Mystic Mog back. He had
promised Madame Estella that
when he went to see her next day
he'd have a plan.

It was no good barging into
Banger's house demanding the
return of Mystic Mog. Banger would
be sure to have some excuse. Like
he'd just found her somewhere and
was about to return her. He would
deny all knowledge of the ransom
letter and his dad would believe him.

Oscar knew better than to annoy
Banger's dad. He owned the school
and just recently had threatened
to close it down if Banger didn't
appear to be gaining special gifts.

Oscar had had to work very hard
to convince him that Banger was
making some progress. No, some
way had to be found to catch Banger
in the act.

He thought and thought, then a
plan finally popped into his head.

"Got it," he yelled, and sat down
with a bump. It was a pity he forgot
he was hovering. It was a pity he
missed the chair and sat down on
the kitchen table. It was a pity his
mum was just serving the pudding
at the time. It was a pity it was the
twins' favourite.

"Look at that," they screeched.
"You've just sat in the trifle. Can't you
look where you're putting your big
fat bottom."

"It's not big or fat," said Oscar,
examining his rear.

"But it is covered in cream,"

sighed his mum. "These trousers will have to go in the wash."

"Pity you can't wash that fizziness out of his feet as well," said his dad. "I was looking forward to that trifle."

"Sorry, Dad," grinned Oscar.

CHAPTER EIGHT

"My plan is very simple," Oscar told
the others as they gathered in Madame
Estella's study next day. "But it needs
all of us."

"Now you mudn't do anyding
dangerous, Oscar," sneezed Madame
Estella. "I could jud go to the police
wid this."

"And tell them you've lost a
talking cat?" said Oscar. "They didn't
believe you when you told them
about seeing the U.F.O.s. And, even
if they did believe you, and Banger
was caught, his dad would be furious
and he might try close down the school

again. We can't risk that."

Gnatalie and Wibbly agreed.
"We'll be very careful," they said.
"We'll keep an eye on Banger all day."

It wasn't difficult. Banger spent all day going round the school, boasting.

"I'm going to buy new trainers," he said. "Expensive trainers. Not like these rubbishy ones you wear, Hover Boy. Where did you get them, anyway? Half-price stall at the market?"

Oscar said nothing. That was *exactly* where he had got them. His parents didn't have money for expensive trainers.

Banger was annoyed that Oscar was ignoring him.

"And just look at those jeans. Are they really yours?"

They weren't. Oscar's were still

drying after last night's episode with
the trifle and he was wearing an
old pair of Angie's. They were too
big round the waist and the bottoms
flapped a bit.

"'Course they're mine," muttered
Oscar.

"They look like *girls'* jeans to me,"
sneered Banger. "Imagine wearing
girls' jeans."

"Imagine yourself with a
broken nose," Oscar wanted to say
but he knew Banger just wanted
to get him into trouble, so he
clenched his fists and his teeth and
said nothing.

"Hover Boy, Hover Boy. Scaredy
cat, scaredy cat," taunted Banger.
Then he stopped suddenly and
went a bit red.

"What was that you said about
a cat, Banger?" said Oscar. "You

haven't seen Mystic Mog around lately, have you. She seems to have disappeared."

Banger shook his head quickly. "Stupid name for a cat. Stupid cat. She's probably gone off somewhere and got lost. I certainly don't know anything about it." And he went off hurriedly.

"He knows *exactly* where Mystic Mog is," said Gnatalie. "Go over the plan again, Oscar, so we get it right."

"OK," said Oscar, "Gather round. At seventeen hundred hours minus five we assemble behind the school wall, near the gate."

"Seventeen hundred hours minus five?" said Wibbly. "You mean sixteen fifty-five."

"Or put another way, five to five," said Gnatalie.

"OK, OK," grinned Oscar.
"I was only trying to sound official.
At the appointed time Gnatalie
will look through the wall and
inform us of the approach of the
suspect – i.e. Banger McGrath.
Wibbly will then proceed to read
the suspect's – i.e. Banger's – mind.
Then I will hover up to the top of
the wall and eyeball the suspect.
Is that clear?"

"Yes, but don't you talk funny,"
grinned Gnatalie. "When do we
grab him?"

"As soon as Madame Estella
hands over the envelope with the
money in it."

"Money?" said Wibbly.

"Some old Monopoly money I
found in the caravan," said Oscar.

"I'm so excited," said Gnatalie.
"I can hardly wait for five to five."

"Or sixteen fifty-five," said Wibbly. "Or, put another way, seventeen hundred hours minus five," said Oscar.

CHAPTER NINE

For once the school day went slowly.
Oscar could think of nothing except
catching Banger in the act and
getting Mystic Mog back. He wondered
if Mystic Mog would be upset at what
had happened to her. He'd mentioned
the missing cat at home to Evie and
Angie. This had been a mistake.

"Mrs Mulligan-along-the-road
had a cat that disappeared for ages,
and when she came back her fur
was all gone and you could see
her ribs sticking out," said Evie.

"That's nothing," said Angie.
"Ellie Walker, in our class, moved

house, and her cat kept going back to the old house and got run over by a ten ton cement lorry at the roundabout."

Oscar was just thinking about this, and imagining – with horror – that happening to Mog, when Miss Twitching, the Maths teacher, asked him the answer to problem number three.

"Squashed cat," said Oscar.

Miss Twitching fixed him with her steely gaze. "I don't appear to have a question about squashed cats in my Maths book, Oscar Smith. Do you?"

"Er, not exactly, no," said Oscar and agitatedly hovered into the air.

"And hovering into the air will not help you," said Miss Twitching. "What question are you at?"

"Well," Oscar swallowed hard

and peered down at his notebook.
"I haven't exactly started yet."

"Then you'd better catch up
after school today, hadn't you?"
said Miss Twitching.

Oh no, thought Oscar. Not today
of all days. But it wasn't wise to argue
with Miss Twitching. He bumped
miserably to the ground and said,
"Yes, Miss Twitching."

Banger McGrath smiled nastily.
He liked to see Hover Boy get into
trouble.

"The answer to question number
three is twenty-four litres of petrol,
Miss Twitching," he volunteered.

"Quite right, Banger. Well done."
said his teacher.

Banger smirked all round. This
was going to be a good day for him.

But not for Oscar.

*   *   *

In Professore Allegore's Mind-reading class Oscar did his best to keep his mind a blank. He didn't want the Professore reading it and starting to talk about cats. Any more mention of cats and Banger might realize Oscar was on to him. So he thought about football.

He thought about the impossibility of getting into the school team. They would never let him be goal keeper, that wouldn't be fair. He could hover up and save all the high balls. But he'd be no good in any other position. Imagine trying to kick the ball from three feet up in the air.

"You are not working well today, Oscar," said the Professore. "In fact, as far as I can see, you are not working at all. Too much thinking about football. Report to me after school to catch up."

Oh no, thought Oscar again.
Not today of all days. But it wasn't
wise to argue with Professore
Allegore, either.

"Yes, Professore," he said
miserably.

Banger couldn't believe his
luck. Hover Boy in trouble again.
Wonderful. He grinned at Oscar.
Oscar glared back.

The final straw came that afternoon when Wanda Fonda took the class out to her vegetable plot in the school garden. She'd been working for ages on growing special plants that might help feed the hungry in poorer countries. She was just explaining this when Oscar suddenly hovered up into the air, did a funny zig-zag dance and fell down into the middle of the plants.

"I'm really sorry, Wanda," said Oscar. "I couldn't help it. It just happened. I'll help you straighten up the plants."

Wanda scowled and muttered, "Idiot."

Mr Blister sighed. "I really don't know what's wrong with you today, Oscar. Go back indoors and clean yourself up."

Oscar knew what was wrong with him, but he couldn't tell Mr Blister.

He went back into the school and was heading for the cloakroom when the faint feeling of fizziness started again in his feet. He immediately shot up into the air and cracked his head on the old panel of bells that hung on the wall. The bells had originally been used – when the old house was owned by Madame Estella's wealthy family – to summon servants to stoke up the fire or bring afternoon tea, but they hadn't worked for ages . . . until now.

Ting a ling – a ling – a ling – a ling – a ling . . .

They went on and on and on and wouldn't stop. Oscar thumped on the panel, but that only made things worse. *Ting a ling – a ling – a ling* they went on, louder than ever. Teachers appeared from the surrounding classrooms and found Oscar banging on the bell panel.

"Oscar Smith," they yelled. *"What do you think you're doing? Stop making that racket. We can't hear ourselves speak. Stop these bells right now!"*

"But I didn't . . . I mean I can't . . . I mean how . . ."

The ringing went on and on.

Discoveries were stopped and
everyone held their ears until Mr
Periwinkle, the caretaker, finally
managed to disconnect the bells.

"Well, isn't that amazing," he said.
"In all the years I've been here that's
never happened before."

"And it better not happen again,"
muttered the teachers, glaring at Oscar.

Oscar opened his mouth to protest, then shut it again. What could he say? The school was in chaos and it had been his fault.

Gnatalie and Wibbly looked on sympathetically, but Banger McGrath was delighted.

"Hover Boy's nothing but trouble," he said to anyone who would listen. "I'm going to tell my dad. He'll probably get him expelled."

At last the long school day ended. Oscar caught up with his work for Miss Twitching and Professore Allegore, and went to meet Gnatalie and Wibbly, who were waiting for him in the school hall. Now all they had to do was put Oscar's plan into action.

CHAPTER TEN

It was seventeen hundred hours minus five, or sixteen fifty-five, or, put another way, five to five when the three friends assembled behind the school wall. Madame Estella, wrapped up in scarves and a long hooded cloak, paced anxiously by the school gate, an envelope in her hand.

"I don't like this," she was muttering. "Not one little bit."

"Right," said Oscar. "Action stations, everyone."

Gnatalie screwed up her eyes and looked through the school wall. Two large dogs, walking their owner, went past. Then . . .

"Suspect has just rounded the corner of Beacham Road," she reported. "He is carrying Mystic Mog in a hamper."

Then it was Wibbly's turn. He screwed up his eyes and read Banger's mind.

"Suspect is just deciding what colour laces to get with his new trainers. It's a toss up between black and red or blue and gold."

Then it was Oscar's turn. He hovered to the top of the school wall and peered over. He couldn't believe his eyes. Banger was carrying Mystic Mog all right, but he was dressed in a long overcoat of his dad's and a Mickey Mouse mask.

"What a wally," muttered Oscar. "Come on. Let's get him!"

*   *   *

They gave him two minutes to reach the school gates and Madame Estella. Then they gave him time to say his piece.

"I am a dangerous catnapper," Banger was saying in a big gruff voice, very like his dad's. "Don't mess with me. Just hand over the money, and the cat goes free."

Madame Estella pretended to be terrified and handed over the envelope with the Monopoly money inside. Banger handed over Mystic Mog. The three friends leapt out.

"Gotcha!" they yelled. Gnatalie and Wibbly grabbed Banger's arms while Oscar hovered up and ripped off the mask.

"Waaa," yelled Banger as the elastic twanged off his nose and made his eyes water. "It wasn't me," he wailed, before anyone could say anything.

"I never did nothing. Someone
gave me the cat."

"And the coat and the mask?"
said Oscar.

Madame Estella ignored Banger
and checked that Mystic Mog was
all right. Then she turned to Banger.
The three friends had never seen
her so angry. Her cornflower blue
eyes were cold, and her quiet voice
icy when she spoke.

"You . . ." she said to Banger,
"are the worst boy it has ever been
my misfortune to meet. Worse than
that, you are a stealer of innocent
creatures who have done you no
harm. You are an extorter of money,
a thief, a blackmailer . . ."

And for the next five minutes
the three friends listened in
amazement as she told a quivering
Banger exactly what she thought of

him. This was a Madame Estella they had never seen before.

Gosh, thought Oscar. I hope I never upset Madame Estella.

Wibbly read his mind. "Me neither," he whispered.

Madame Estella was just telling Banger about all the extra homework he would have, and about how he would sweep the school playground twice a day for the next month when a large silver Rolls-Royce drew up, and Banger's dad got out. As usual he was dressed in a sharp suit which strained across his large chest. As usual he glittered with more gold than a jeweller's window. As usual he had his gold tooth with the diamond in it clamped on to a fat cigar.

"Ah," he said. "I see Boris Junior has returned that idiot cat of yours that got itself lost in the park, Madame

Estella. Good thing he spotted it.
I hope you gave him a suitable
reward for his trouble."

"Indeed I did, Mr McGrath,
and I should like to add that he
grows more and more like his father
every day."

Boris senior beamed and clapped
a hand on Banger's shoulder.

"You mark my words," he said. "This boy will go far."

"But not far enough," muttered Oscar.

"Now perhaps," said Madame Estella sweetly, "you'd like to take your son home. I think I've said all I need to say to him for the present, but I shall be taking a very keen interest in him, and keeping a very close eye on him, in the future."

Banger escaped into his father's car as fast as he could and the Rolls-Royce purred away.

Something else purred too. Mystic Mog. She leapt into Oscar's arms and said something that sounded very like, "What's a cat got to do to get some cookies around here?"

Madame Estella laughed and said,

"Mystic Mog's obviously none the worse for her adventure. This way for the lemonade and cookies, everyone."

Mystic Mog snuggled up to Oscar and said, "Well done, Hover Boy."

Then Oscar could have sworn she added, "My hero."

Oscar blushed to the tips of his ears, then thought, Don't be so silly, Oscar. Out loud he said, "You really are an extraordinary cat, Mog."

Everyone else grinned. "But no more extraordinary than Hover Boy!"

MORE ADVENTURES FOR . . .

FIZZY FEET

THE FIRST HOVER BOY STORY!

Hovering is fun, but being different
sometimes makes Oscar feel lonely.
At his ordinary school, he has to hide
his special talent. But when he gets caught
by his teacher Miss Cheevers, and is
sent to see the head, his life soon changes
for ever . . .

Next day, he starts at the School Of
Greatly Gifted Youth. It's fantastic making
new friends and discoveries, but it's not long
before Oscar learns that his problems
are far from over . . .

MORE ADVENTURES FOR . . .

BEAT THE BULLY

THE SECOND HOVER BOY STORY!

Bully boy Banger McGrath has it in
for Oscar from almost the minute Oscar
arrives at S.O.G.G.Y. What makes it worse
is that Banger's dad owns the school.
If Banger doesn't learn a special
gift of his own, his dad will close
S.O.G.G.Y down.

Can Oscar, Gnatalie and Wibbly think of
a way to solve the problem? Even if it means
telling everyone about Oscar's special gift . . .

ABOUT THE AUTHOR

MARGARET RYAN

was born and brought up in Paisley,
Scotland, in a house full of books.
She enjoyed writing, too, but didn't
become a full-time writer until she had
married and had brought up her two
children, and been a teacher. Then, one
day, she saw an advertisement in her local
paper for a writers' group and joined up.
Her writing career began!

Since then, Margaret has published
many bestselling books for children of all
ages, and in 2000, she won a Scottish
Arts Council Book Award. Today she loves
meeting her readers and is greatly in
demand for her lively storytelling sessions.
She lives with her husband in an old mill
just outside St Andrews. The area is rich
in wildlife, which Margaret hopes will
be a great source of ideas . . .